ATOS Book Level: _____ 4.5 _____
AR Points: _____ 1.0 _____
Quiz #: 132467 ☑RP ☐ LS ☐ VP
Lexile: _____

For Roddy —A. L.
For Coco —R. H.

First published in the United States in 2009 by Chronicle Books LLC.

North American type design by Molly Baker.
Typeset in Berkeley.
Manufactured in China.

Library of Congress Cataloging-in-Publication Data
Lester, Alison.
[Saving Mr. Pinto]
The Royal Show / by Alison Lester ; illustrated by Roland Harvey.
p. cm. — (Horse crazy ; bk. 4)
Summary: On the way to assist their riding teacher at the Royal Show, Bonnie and
Sam find a starving pony that they feel must try to rescue.
ISBN 978-0-8118-6941-6
[1. Horses—Fiction. 2. Horse shows—Fiction. 3. Animal rescue—Fiction. 4.
Australia—Fiction.] I. Harvey, Roland, ill. II. Title. III. Series.
PZ7.L56284Rp 2009
[Fic]—dc22
2008052606

10 9 8 7 6 5 4 3 2 1

Chronicle Books LLC
680 Second Street, San Francisco, California 94107

www.chroniclekids.com

HORSE
crazy

THE ROYAL SHOW **4**

by Alison Lester

illustrated by Roland Harvey

chronicle books · san francisco

Winter

Neither Bonnie nor Sam had their own pony but they managed to ride almost every day. They kept an eye on all the horses in town. Now, in winter, when the days were short and the nights were long and cold, Bonnie and Sam were always busy after school.

They stopped at Tarzan's paddock first.
Tarzan was the grumpiest pony in town but
he knew Bonnie and Sam always brought him
a treat to make him happy.

"Look at you," said Sam as he picked up her
apple core with his whiskery lips. "You look like
a doormat, you're so hairy."

"That's right," said Bonnie, scratching his ear.
"You don't even need a rug."

Bella

Whale

Next they visited big Whale, who shared a paddock with tiny Bella, then Blondie and Tex behind the newsstand, and Horrie the old racehorse, who loved a relaxing neck massage.

Blondie

Tex

Horrie

Tricky

They stopped to check on their friend
Tricky, who Bonnie once rode in a circus. Sam
straightened his rug and Bonnie threw him
a biscuit of hay from the shed.

Then they skipped along under the leaden
winter sky, jumping to keep warm and dodging
the puddles in the street. The paddocks were
bare, with clumps of jonquils and daffodils
scattered over them. The deciduous trees
had lost all their leaves. It was a cold,
gray landscape.

Rugs and Rubs

The last stop before they reached Sam's house was to visit Biscuit, a nervous chestnut mare who belonged to Wally Webster, the local stock agent. Biscuit would have frozen without the girls. Her coat was fine and she shivered in the cold weather, but Wally refused to buy a rug for her. "It makes as much sense as putting a pair of pants on a seagull," he had snorted. "Horses have fur. They don't need overcoats."

"Actually, they have hair, not fur," Sam had whispered to Bonnie as Wally sloshed away through the puddles. They didn't want to be too rude to Wally because he let them ride Biscuit whenever they liked.

When Bonnie and Sam had told their riding instructor about Biscuit, she had given the girls an old rug, and now Biscuit was snug in a bright purple coat. While Bonnie gave Biscuit some hay, Sam felt around the mare's shoulders and wither, checking for rubs.

"Right as rain," she said to Bonnie. "I'll race you to the house!"

An Offer

Sam slurped her hot chocolate and looked out the window at Drover sheltering from the wind behind the shed in her paddock. Sam's family was just her and her dad. Bill was the local policeman and Drover was his horse.

The phone rang. "Better not answer," Sam said. "It'll be your mom, wanting to pick you up."

Bonnie lived on a big farm out of town. If she didn't go straight home on the school bus, her parents had to drive in from Peppermint Plain to collect her. As she went to Sam's house nearly every night after school, this meant a lot of trips for Chester and Woo. But it wasn't Woo on the phone. It was their riding instructor.

"Yep, yep, sure. Yes, we can come right away." Bonnie hung up the receiver. "That was Cheryl," she said, her voice excited. "She wants us to go to her place *now*. She's got an offer for us."

Cheryl Smythe-Tyght lived with her mother and an elderly blue heeler, called Burl Ives, on the outskirts of Currawong Creek. Everybody called their farm Tidytown because it was so neat: white fences, red sheds, green grass, straight rows of trees, and a smooth gravel drive that Bonnie and Sam raced up. Sam's little dog, Pants, ran ahead. Pants was short for Smartie Pants, because she thought she knew everything.

Cheryl's beautiful dressage horse, Chocolate Charm, nickered to them from the open stable door. He was covered in rugs, so only his ears, eyes, and nose could be seen.

"Hi, Choco!" they called to him. From time to time the girls picked up horse poo in his paddock and Cheryl paid them in riding lessons. Riding Choco was different from riding any other horse. He was big, powerful, graceful, and had beautiful manners as well. When they rode Choco they felt like princesses.

"How are my two lovely girls?" called Cheryl's mother. Kath had ridden show horses all her life and she liked anyone who loved horses as much as she did. She hugged them both into her fluffy purple cardigan with white stallions embroidered on it. "Come on, Cheryl," she said impatiently. "Ask them!"

Cheryl looked at Bonnie and Sam very seriously. "What I'm going to ask you will be fun, but it's also hard, responsible work." Bonnie looked at Sam and tried not to laugh. She always got the giggles when anybody gave her a talking to. But Cheryl said, "I'm going to the Royal Show next week. Mom's sister, Aunty Lil, usually comes and helps Mom strap for me, but she's broken her wrist and I need some extra help." She looked at them both for a long time and Bonnie had to fight the giggles again. "Would you two like to come and help?"

"Woohoo! Woohoo!" yelled Bonnie and Sam. They had dreamed of going to the Royal Show since they were little girls. "YES!" they both shouted at once.

"There's something else." Cheryl put her finger up, to quiet them.

"I entered you in the Royal Show Junior Girl Rider, Bonnie, ages ago, after you won at the Gardenhope Show."

Best Junior
Girl Rider

Every summer and autumn, Cheryl and Kath
traveled to agricultural shows around the
country, competing in hack and riding classes.
Cheryl's purple four-wheel drive towed
a matching purple horse float.
Sometimes Bonnie and Sam
went to help, and occasionally
Cheryl let the girls enter
a riding class on Choco.
Bonnie always did better
than Sam, even though
Sam was a good rider.

"It's just because I'm small, Sam," Bonnie said to cheer her friend up, and that was part of it. Bonnie looked like a sprite on Choco. But she also had a grace and magic that made her stand out. "Star quality," Cheryl called it. When Bonnie won Best Junior Girl Rider at the Gardenhope Show, she was ecstatic about her lovely blue sash. Sam clapped until her hands were sore. Neither of them realized that Bonnie's win had qualified her to ride at the Royal Show.

Now, Bonnie felt excited and scared at the same time. Sam felt a twinge of envy, then pushed it behind her and they both screamed with happiness.

"Next week Mom and I will go to the showgrounds and get Choco settled in," said Cheryl. "I've asked your folks to let you miss the last day of school so you can catch the train into the city. Mrs. Puller is bringing one of her cakes to the show and she said she'll look after you." She smiled. "I need you then because Choco and I are riding in the Garryowen."

"Mom will tell you about the Garryowen," Cheryl said in response to the girls' raised eyebrows. "She's ridden in it heaps of times. I'm going to feed Choco."

Kath pulled down a cracked photo album and flipped through it. "Look, here I am at my very first Garryowen, forty years ago." Bonnie and Sam peered at the black-and-white photograph of Kath, looking more like Cheryl, on a tall gray horse. "That's old Overlander. He was my first hack."

"What is the Garryowen, Kath?" asked Sam.

"Well," said Kath, "it's a competition for the lady rider and her horse, for the best in the land. There are six judges giving marks for saddlery, general appearance, rider's costume, riding, horse's manners and paces, and horse's confirmation and soundness. Everything has to be perfect."

"Why is it called the Garryowen?" asked Bonnie. "What does it mean?"

"I think it's a famous Irish marching tune, but it was also the name of a horse. Garryowen was

a beautiful hack owned by a famous rider called
Violet Murrell, who lived about seventy years
ago. That's before even *I* was born. One night
Violet woke to find the stables on fire with her
horses all trapped inside, including her favorite,
Garryowen. She died trying to get them out and
the horses all died too, and I think her husband
and their little dog died later." Kath wiped a tear
away. "They started the Garryowen in memory
of Violet and her courage."

19

On the Train

Bonnie and Sam waved to Woo as the train creaked slowly out of Baxter Station. The railway line didn't go as far as Currawong Creek, so Woo had driven Mrs. Puller and the girls to catch the train at Baxter.

"See you next week!" Woo called to them. Pants looked at them sadly from the car. She hated to be left behind.

Mrs. Puller held her cake tin tightly on her lap. At every Royal Show for the last fifteen years she had won a prize for her fruit cake. She was famous in Currawong Creek for her fantastic wedding cakes. Now she stared at Bonnie and Sam through her pointy glasses.

"You won't misbehave, will you?" she said. "I'm not used to children. Mr. Puller and I were never blessed with little ones."

Sam felt awkward. She knew Mr. Puller had

died last year and she didn't know what to say, but Bonnie leapt right in. Woo had taught Bonnie that people like to talk about their loved ones.

"No, Mrs. Puller, we'll be good," said Bonnie. "Tell us about Mr. Puller. Did he used to go to the show with you?"

It was as though Bonnie had unplugged Mrs. Puller. Story after story came tumbling out: the time Mr. Puller won the wood chopping contest, when Mr. Puller dropped the cake, Mr. Puller and the runaway pig, and Mr. Puller's pasta disaster.

In the City

Bonnie and Sam's eyes were popping out of their heads as the train passed through the city. In Currawong Creek everybody looked pretty much the same, but here the streets were crowded with people of all shapes and sizes, wearing clothes and hairstyles that might have been from another planet. The train moved on again, wobbling across a mesh of silver tracks.

"We'll be there soon," said Mrs. Puller. "Make sure you've got all your bags. I know how forgetful you young people can be."

Just before the showgrounds, the train stopped to let another train past. Sam stared idly at the leaning fence beside the railway tracks. Bulging graffiti spelled something she couldn't read. It was everywhere, writing you couldn't understand. Bonnie was thinking the same thing.

"It's like yelling but not saying anything," she said. "Maybe it's a secret language that only the graffiti writers know."

Suddenly Sam saw something move behind
the fence. "Look, Bon! There's a pony in that
backyard!"

Bonnie leapt to the window so she could
see through the gap in the fence. The pony took
a step forward and they could both see it clearly—
a tiny gray thing, with all his ribs showing.

"He's starving!" Bonnie's voice cracked with
emotion at the sight of the poor pony. He had
a dirty rope tied around his neck.

24

"He's tied up to the clothes line, Bon," said Sam. "Look, you can see the top of the laundry hoist above the fence."

Mrs. Puller wriggled over so she could see, too. She didn't let go of her cake tin.

"Oh, the poor little thing," she cried. "Who could treat an animal so badly?"

The Royal Show

Mrs. Puller led Bonnie and Sam through the showgrounds. She knew all the streets and alleys by heart. Music blared and motors roared as they walked past the sideshows. There were so many different noises competing that it was impossible to hear anything.

Carnival workers shouted, advertising their games; toys and show bags fluttered in the breeze; and people on the swing carousel screamed above them.

Gradually they left the noise behind them as they circled behind the huge grandstand of the main arena. The Ferris wheel loomed high above pavilions where all sorts of agricultural produce were displayed. The streets thronged with farmers leading their cattle and horses to the judging arena.

"That's where I'll be taking my cake." Mrs. Puller pointed to a pavilion down a cobbled street. "And here you are." She led the girls past a long building where horses poked their heads out the stable doors. At the end, Sam could see a purple horse rug.

"That has to be Choco," she said to Bonnie.

• • •

"Kath! Kath!" Bonnie couldn't tell the story of the poor starving pony quickly enough. Her words came out so fast that Kath couldn't understand anything. Finally, she sat on her bag and took some deep breaths while Sam explained what they had seen. Kath was like Bonnie's Aunt Birdy—she always listened and didn't treat them like little kids.

"Oh, dear," said Kath, her blue eyes filling with tears. "It sounds like a very bad situation." She hugged the girls close. "That little pony needs rescuing. Let me think about things for a while."

Sam felt as though a heavy load had been taken from her. She wished her dad was there, but if Kath said she'd think about the pony, she would, and maybe she'd know what to do.

"Cheryl's gone to buy some extra horse shampoo," said Kath. "So it's up to me to welcome you to Paris." She made a bow. "Come in, ladies, to your home away from home."

29

Paris

The horses and riders competing at the Royal Show stayed at the showgrounds for ten days. Every afternoon at three o'clock they all took part in the Grand Parade.

"Everybody has to be in it," explained Kath.

The horses lived in stables and the people lived nearby in tiny rooms called lockers. At the end of each stable block were communal bathrooms and toilets. Kath and Cheryl had been coming to the show for forty years and they always stayed in the same locker. They called it Paris, because it had a tiny square of lawn and a plum tree in front of it. Choco's stable was right next door. Cheryl and Kath had set up a card table with an electric kettle and frying pan and some camping chairs.

"We've got folding beds," said Kath. "We'll sleep down here. Your bedroom is upstairs.

And look . . ." She kneeled beside the wall and pointed to a wobbly drawing. "Cheryl drew this little horse when she was four."

Bonnie and Sam climbed up the rickety ladder, spread their sleeping bags out on the airbeds Cheryl had blown up, and unpacked their things, turning the tiny space into home.

"Look, Sam. We've got a window." Bonnie released the latch and looked down the sloping roof to the street below. "It's like a little town. I can't wait to explore."

Suddenly something banged the floor from below. It was Kath, with a broom.

"I have a plan, girls," she called. "Come down and I'll explain it."

. . .

"Ssshhhh! We have to be as silent as wolves."
Kath crept along in the shadow of the
grandstand, Burl Ives at her heels. She was
dressed in black, like a cat burglar. Bonnie
and Sam wore trousers and parkas over their
pajamas, with beanies to keep their heads warm.
It was so cold their teeth were chattering.

Sam looked back over her shoulder. If Cheryl
knew what they were up to, she'd be furious.
But this was Kath's solution to the problem
of the neglected pony, and Bonnie and Sam
weren't going to argue. None of them could
bear the thought of the little pony spending one
more day in misery, yet they were all aware of
Cheryl's big event in two days time.

"We can't tell her," Kath had said. "It will
ruin everything for her. She won't be able to
concentrate on Choco and the Garryowen if she
knows about the pony."

Cheryl slept like a log, so once she began to
snore that night, Kath shook the girls awake and
they set off to save the pony.

Bonnie reckoned the backyard was only about a hundred yards away from the showgrounds station. A well-trodden path ran through the long grass that grew against the back fences and they padded along it like robbers in the night, following Kath's downturned flashlight.

"This is it," whispered Sam, pointing to the silver graffiti reflecting in the moonlight. She peered through the fence into the backyard. The house was dark.

"Yes! There he is!" Kath wriggled beside her and Bonnie smelled the Chanel perfume that she always wore. Burl Ives pushed up to the gap too, whining.

"Oh, the poor little thing!" sighed Kath.

"Can we just take him?" whispered Bonnie. "Isn't that stealing?"

"I'd call it a rescue," said Kath. "No pony deserves to be kept in these terrible conditions. Let's see if we can untie his rope . . ."

Panic!

WOOF! WOOF! WOOF!

A black shape hurtled across the yard, barking furiously at them. Burl Ives ran yelping into the night. Kath and Bonnie and Sam raced back along the track, trying not to scream, tripping and stumbling in their panic.

Suddenly a light flooded the yard and the huge shadow of a man spread out. "Get out! Go on! Get!" The dog kept barking, a savage, growling bark that sounded like a wild beast.

The man shouted a long, loud burst of angry swear words, and the three horse rescuers and their dog ran on without looking back.

In the safety of the showgrounds, they stopped running. Kath bent over, her hands on her knees, wheezing like a steam train. Burl Ives was panting just as loudly.

"Are you okay, Kath?" Sam asked.

Bonnie was worried, too. "I didn't know old people could run that fast," she said, and Kath's wheezing turned into whoops of laughter.

"Yes," she said, between breaths. "I'm, GASP, pretty fit, GASP, for an old girl."

When they turned down their street they could see a light on in Paris and they knew they were in trouble.

"You WHAT?" Cheryl's eyebrows shot up in shock when she heard where they had been. She waggled her finger at Kath. "You are the most irresponsible old lady in the world!"

Bonnie and Sam sat very still on the camping chairs, not daring to look at one another in case they got the giggles, while Kath told Cheryl the whole story. To their surprise Cheryl calmed down.

"It's very sweet that you didn't want to worry

me because of the Garryowen, but I would rather
know than have you sneaking around in the dark."
She turned the electric kettle on. "I shampooed
Choco twice today. He's so clean you could eat
off him. All I have to do tomorrow is give him a
light workout and ride in the Grand Parade." She
spooned cocoa into the mugs. "I'll have plenty of
time to help rescue the clothesline pony."

A Bird's-Eye View

Bonnie and Sam held on tight to the metal bar
as the Ferris wheel took them slowly up into the
sky. First they could see the showgrounds, then
they could see the streets outside, then they
could see the whole city. The big wheel stopped
to let more passengers on and Bonnie and Sam

swayed like two perching pigeons, right at the
top. The train line snaked away toward the city.

"Bon!" Sam pointed. "There's the pony." The
unhappy pony stood, head down in a muddy,
messy backyard. He looked very sad.

"And, Sam," said Bonnie, "you can see which house
it is. It's that blue house with a pile of bricks in the
front yard, in the next street along from the station."

"I'm coming! Stop that knockin'!"

Fatty Phillips pushed open his front door and blinked into the bright winter light. Two little girls and two women stood on the front step.

"Waddaya want?" he said. "I'm not buyin' nothing."

Cheryl got straight to the point. "We're not selling anything." She looked him right in the eye. "On the contrary. We would like to buy something from *you*."

Kath pushed forward like a terrier. "We know you have an ill-treated pony in your backyard and we wish to buy it. If you don't agree right now to a reasonable price we'll phone the RSPCA!"

Fatty scratched his hairy belly. He had no money and no chance of getting any until next week. He didn't have to think for long.

"Deal done," he said. "Give me three hundred dollars and the critter's yours."

"Two hundred," countered Cheryl, and Kath's glare told Fatty to accept. He led them down the side of his house, past bursting bags of garbage and piles of beer bottles. They had to wait while he locked the growling dog in the house.

The pony nickered when he saw them and Kath turned on the man.

"How could you starve a pony like this?" Cheryl untied the dirty rope. "What are you doing with it?" she asked him.

To their surprise, tears welled in his eyes. "I bought it from a fella at the pub. I thought my ex was bringing the kids down from Queensland and I wanted to surprise them." He looked down at his dirty moccasins. "But they never came. I don't know nothin' about horses. He ate all the grass in the first week and after that I've been feeding him bread."

He followed them out to the street. "I didn't know," he said hopelessly.

"Ignorance is no excuse," said Kath. She handed him two hundred dollars as Cheryl led the pony away. "I should report you to the police!"

41

A Surprise

While Cheryl exercised Choco and Kath had
a lie down, Bonnie and Sam took the pony to
the washing bay.

"He's a pinto!" Sam said in surprise as the
mud washed off him. The pony was quiet and
well-mannered.

"He's somebody's pet, Sam," said Bonnie.
"He must be stolen." It took three shampoos to
get all the dirt out of his coat and finally he was
sparkling black-and-white.

"Let's call him Mr. Pinto," said Sam.

While Mr. Pinto munched on hay in Choco's stable, Sam towelled him dry and Bonnie combed the knots out of his mane and tail. Every once in a while he reached around and nudged her with his nose.

"I think he likes us," said Bonnie.

"He's got a heart-marking under his tummy, Bon," Sam said, as she lay on her back, drying underneath him.

"Any room for us in there?" asked Cheryl. She led Choco into the stable and let him sniff the pony. Neither horse squealed or struck out. "I think it's love at first sight," said Cheryl. "I was going to find a spare stable, but maybe he can share with Choco."

Kath cooked fried eggs and bacon for dinner that night and they went to bed early. Tomorrow, Cheryl was riding in the Garryowen and the alarm clock was set for four o'clock in the morning. As Bonnie and Sam drifted into sleep, fireworks exploding over the main arena lit up the loft.

Not a Hair Out of Place

Bonnie and Sam worked like little ants, passing, fetching, carrying, holding, and helping. Choco was like a great big bride with everybody fussing over him. Cheryl braided his mane and tail so not a hair was out of place. She tied the braids in place with matching thread. Kath wiped every inch of him with a fine cloth, polished his hooves black, and even cleaned his teeth. There was not a speck of dust in his coat. Mr. Pinto stood quietly in the corner chewing hay. Now and again he smirked at Choco as if to say, *Man! You look ridiculous.*

"Look at these rules." Bonnie flipped through the Garryowen guidebook. "The lining of your jacket has to be navy, you have to have cufflinks with chains, a white lace-edged hanky in your left-hand waist pocket, your spur has to sit on the stitching of your boot. . . . How do you keep track of all this stuff?"

At six o'clock the street sweepers went past and the girls stopped for breakfast. Soon Choco was saddled and it was Cheryl's turn to get ready. Her clothes came out of their plastic covers and Kath dressed her like a doll.

Finally Cheryl was ready and swung onto Choco. Kath inspected horse and rider carefully, searching for flaws.

"You look fabulous," she said. "Good luck and have a great time."

Bonnie and Sam ran ahead of Choco as he walked toward the main arena, then waved as he walked through the gates.

"Good luck, Choco! Good luck, Cheryl!"

Kath, Bonnie, and Sam sat high in the grandstand and watched Cheryl and Choco go through their paces. There were ten horses lined up and they all looked absolutely perfect.

"There's another two groups to be judged after this, thirty riders altogether, but they judge them in groups of ten," Kath explained. "When I used to compete . . ."

"In the olden days," Sam joked, and Kath gave her a play punch.

"Yes, in the olden days. This was a huge event. Sometimes there were more than a hundred competitors and we all lined up together. If you were at the end of the line, you had to wait for hours and you'd certainly lost your sparkle by the time your turn came. That's why they judge it in groups now."

One by one the riders completed their workout, following the judge's instructions and showing off their horses. Round circles, square halts, extended trots, and flying changes looked easy and effortless. Choco did everything perfectly.

When it was time for Cheryl's costume to be marked, she dismounted and stood on a square of canvas. Bonnie and Sam couldn't help laughing as the judge carefully inspected every inch of her. "She's even looking in her ears," whispered Sam. Two judges checked Choco and his gear just as thoroughly.

Finally the judges lined the horses up and they stood as still as statues. Only Choco moved, turning his head slightly toward the stables.

"He's thinking about that little pony," Kath said. "Oh, dear. They'll mark him down for that."

No Prize for Chocko

"We are really sorry, Cheryl," said Sam. "We didn't mean to mess up your Garryowen." Bonnie and Sam felt terrible.

"That's right, love." Kath felt guilty, too. "If we had left that pony where he was you would have been placed for sure. You might even have won."

Cheryl was snipping the thread from Choco's braids, undoing hours of work in a few minutes.

"I can't pretend I'm not disappointed. But I'm disappointed with *him*." She slapped Choco on the neck. "He's the big baby who should have behaved better." She teased out the braids with her fingers and Choco's mane stuck out in curls. "I hope you feel as stupid as you look," she said to him. "I'll just have to work harder for next year. But we did the right thing. We had to save Mr. Pinto. I'm not sorry about that." She turned to the girls. "Now we have to figure out what to do with him."

Bonnie had a plan already. "Let's make a found poster, and stick it to the stable door. He must belong to somebody."

Bonnie and Sam worked on the poster together.

"That looks exactly like him!" Cheryl said. "Make sure you put our address here at the show on it. I'll get some copies made at the office and you can stick them up around the showgrounds."

Later the girls set off to put up posters.
They took turns riding Sam's skateboard, with
Burl Ives pulling them along. There wasn't
much asphalt in Currawong Creek, but here
at the showgrounds the streets were made for
skateboarding.

They stopped to watch the performing pigs
and bought show bags and cotton candy. At
the animal nursery they fed a baby lamb and
cuddled collie pups.

That afternoon hundreds of people stopped by
their stable to look at Mr. Pinto, but nobody knew
where he was from. One shifty-looking man tried

to claim him, but he didn't know what the pony's secret marking was. And when Cheryl questioned him, he backed into the crowd and ran away.

Just as they were about to shut the stable door and play a game of Scrabble, a couple stopped to read the poster. The man had a large camera and the woman reached through the door to shake Kath's hand.

"I'm Gloria Gold, from the *Daily News*," she said. "I think we have tomorrow's front page story here."

Front Page News

The next day Bonnie and Sam jumped out of bed as soon as the alarm went off and got Burl Ives to tow them to the corner store so they could buy the paper.

"Look, Kath! Cheryl!" They burst into the locker. "We're on the front page!" The photo took up half the front page of the *Daily News*—Bonnie and Sam on either side of Mr. Pinto, just their faces filling the picture.

"DO YOU KNOW THIS PONY?" screamed the headline. The text below told the story and described Bonnie and Sam as "plucky youngsters." Kath and Cheryl read the article, then tore the page out and stuck it on the wall of the locker.

"Well," said Cheryl, "that's your fifteen minutes of fame. We've forgotten something though. Tomorrow is your riding class, Bonnie. We have to get you and Choco ready for the Junior Girl Rider."

Sam watched while Bonnie trotted Choco around the practice arena. The small enclosure was crowded with riders trying to exercise their horses. They all went clockwise, then, when a bell rang, they all turned and went counter-clockwise. Cheryl stood at the fence, calling instructions to Bonnie as she rode past.

"Heels down . . . that's good . . . more contact." When a fat appaloosa kicked out at Choco, Bonnie slowed and rode out the gate. "Why are you stopping?" Cheryl asked. "You both need more work."

"I'm sorry, Cheryl." Sam could see tears in Bonnie's eyes. "I don't like riding in such a crowd. Everyone is so pushy. Maybe I'm not cut out to be a show rider."

But the next day Bonnie bravely rode out onto the main arena. "She's going to do well," Cheryl said. "I can feel it in my bones."

"And look at Choco," Sam added. "He looks beautiful. Perhaps he's trying to make up for the Garryowen."

The thirty competitors in the Junior Girl Rider event rode around the judge in a circle.

"This is where showmanship comes in," Kath said. "If you get stuck on the outside, the judge doesn't even see you."

The judge called riders in one by one and finally everybody was lined up. Then it was time for the workout, and each rider did the same routine, finishing with an extended canter across the arena. Some of the horses took off like rockets, then didn't want to stop, but Choco's canter was flawless. He moved smoothly into a fast, powerful stride and then eased into a soft, square halt right on the finish line. Bonnie sat on him lightly, and her legs and hands didn't move. Sam knew she would be talking to him in silent horse talk.

When the judge lined the riders up, Bonnie and Choco won first place. Sam, Kath, and Cheryl stood up and clapped. Bonnie bowed to the judge and cantered a lap of honor around the arena, her blue sash shining in the sun.

TV Too!

Bonnie rode Choco into the
stable, Kath shut the door,
and the four of them jumped
up and down, grinning and
squealing. Bonnie was so
excited she couldn't speak, so
Kath had to phone Chester and Woo to tell
them the good news. Cheryl pinned the blue
sash above the stable door.

Suddenly there was a knock on the door.
"Hello! Hello! Are the girls who saved the pony
there?"

A group of people peered into the locker.
One man had a movie camera and a glamorous
woman held up a fluffy microphone.

"Hello there! I'm Sally Starlight from *It's Your
Tonight*." Her blonde hair looked like a golden
helmet. "Can we interview you about the pony?"

They crowded into the stable and set up the camera and lights. Bonnie and Sam told their story, but when Mr. Pinto tried to eat her hair, Sally Starlight said they had enough footage.

"Thanks, ladies," she said. "And make sure you watch the show tonight."

Later that afternoon Bonnie rode Choco in the Grand Parade, her winner's sash tied across her chest. Sam led Mr. Pinto in the parade as well, and Sally Starlight and her team shot more footage of them. The horses were paraded in small circles in the middle of the arena, and the sheep and cattle made a big circle around them. Right out on the trotting track, the harness horses and Brewery Clydesdales made the biggest circle of all. Everybody did ten laps of the arena and the spectators in the grandstands clapped and cheered.

That night they went to Kath's friend's locker. Marnie had a portable TV and they snuggled in to watch themselves on *It's Your Tonight*.

"This will find Mr. Pinto's family," said Sam. "Everybody watches this show."

While they waited for the program to start, Bonnie flipped through Marnie's copy of *Horse Deals*.

"Mr. Pinto was in here!" she said suddenly.
"In *Horse Deals*. Remember, Sam? When we were
at Janice's newsstand last summer?"

"That's right," said Sam. "You noticed him
because he looked like a black-and-white
version of Bella. Let's call them tomorrow."

"Here we go." Marnie turned the volume up
and Sally Starlight's up-and-down reporter's
voice filled the little room.

Pokey Packer

Before Bonnie and Sam had a chance to call
Horse Deals magazine the next day, the TV
crew was back at Paris. Somebody, who knew
somebody, who knew the family that owned
Mr. Pinto, saw the story on *It's Your Tonight*
and put them in touch with the TV station.
The network helicopter had flown up to the
mountains where the family lived, and now
it landed at the showgrounds heliport. The
cameras rolled as Mr. and Mrs. Packer and
their little girl Helen raced up to peer over the
stable door.

"It's him!" Helen squealed. "It's Pokey! Oh, Pokey, I've missed you."

Pokey Packer had been stolen from his paddock a year ago and now he could go home. Kath made cups of tea and the Packers showed them photos of Pokey, and thanked the horse rescuers for their fine work. They insisted on giving Kath the two hundred dollars she'd paid to get Pokey.

"Do you know his secret marking?" Sam asked Helen. She nodded.

"Yes, I do." Helen traced a heart on the wall with her finger.

Back to
Currawong Creek

Burl Ives sat between Bonnie and Sam on the
back seat of Cheryl's four-wheel drive, making
such bad smells they had to keep the windows
down. Behind them in the horse trailer, Choco
munched hay. Pokey Packer was on his way
back to the mountains.

The city turned into suburbs and the suburbs thinned and became countryside. Sam turned to Bonnie.

"I can't wait to see Dad and Pants," she said. "And I wonder how all the horses are."

"I'm missing Mom and Dad, too," Bonnie replied. "The show was fun, but it will be nice to be back at Currawong Creek."

GLOSSARY OF AUSTRALIAN TERMS

Biscuit of hay

noun: a 1-to 2-inch-thick layer of hay from a bale

Blue heeler

noun: a dog that guides livestock by nipping at their heels

Drover

noun: someone who herds sheep or cattle

Hack

noun: a horse meant for saddle riding

Strapping

verb: grooming a horse, especially after exercise